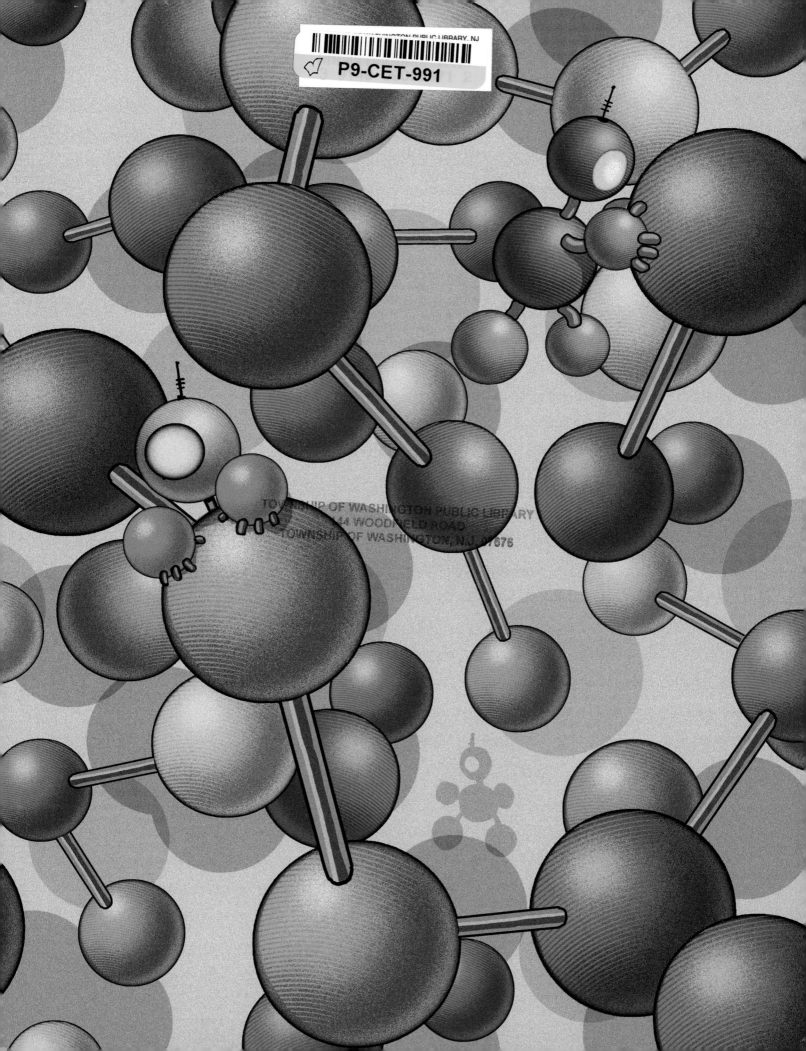

Little, Brown and Company
Hachette Book Group
1290 Avenue of the Americas, New York, NY 10104
Visit us at lb-kids.com

Little, Brown and Company is a division of Hachette Book Group, Inc. • The Little, Brown name and logo are trademarks of Hachette Book Group, Inc. • The publisher is not responsible for websites (or their content) that are not owned by the publisher. • First Edition: August 2016 • Library of Congress Cataloging-in-Publication Data • Gall, Chris, author, illustrator. • NanoBots / Chris Gall.—First edition • pages cm • Summary: A young inventor accidentally creates a group of tiny robots that employ their unique abilities and teamwork to become incredibly useful—and maybe even change the world. Includes author's note on the science and uses of nano-robotics. • ISBN 978-0-316-37552-8 (hardcover) • [1. Robots—Fiction. 2. Size—Fiction.] 1. Title. • PZ7.G1352Nan 2016 • [E]—dc23 • 2015007825 • 10 9 8 7 6 5 4 3 2 1 • APS • PRINTED IN CHINA

For George N.—
You made it all happen.

ROBOT CONSTRUCTION KIT
INSTRUCTIONS INSIDE

The illustrations for this book were created in Adobe Creative Suite with a Wacom drawing tablet. This book was edited by Andrea Spooner and designed by Tracy Shaw and Phil Caminiti. The production was supervised by Erika Schwartz, and the production editor was Andy Ball. This book was printed on 128 gsm Gold Sun matte. The text was set in Binary ITC.

BOX 2
UP

SHRINK WRAP

LATE ONE NIGHT, deep down in a musty basement, a great inventor set out to build the most incredible robots the world had ever seen. But to his surprise, his finished creations were so tiny that some could only be seen with a microscope. The inventor called them **NANOBOTS**, which means "tiny robots," and he gave each his or her own special power. "These NanoBots will change the world!" he declared.

NOTES
seem smaller
usual robots
I hope.

Soon, the inventor realized the NanoBots could fit in places that bigger robots could not.

Take a look at these **SeekerBots** —they explore unseen worlds. They love meeting strange new creatures, such as the nearly invisible beings living in a drop of pond water. They've never met an amoeba they didn't like.

HELOBOTS fly in great swarms, like tiny bees. When they stick together, they can form any shape they want. Look up in the sky! You might see HeloBots racing to help.

CHEWBOTS love to gobble nasty, icky stuff. They can never get enough! No matter how dirty a room gets, they'll make it squeaky clean. They even eat the gum the inventor tracked on the carpet. *SNARFLE, WARFLE, CHOMPLE, BUUUURP!*

MEDIBOT knows every nook and cranny inside the inventor's body. She does her best work inside his nose, keeping out germy invaders. MediBot makes sure they *NEVER* have an appointment.

Meet **Lady Lance-o-Bot**! She is the noble knight of the garden. She keeps watch over the inventor's super solar greenhouse. Those foul dragons had better watch their step—or they might lose an antenna!

If you're afraid of the dark, never fear! GUARDOBOTS will watch over you. They use force fields to keep any bedroom safe from goblins, monsters, and under-the-bedders. Pleasant dreams, everyone!

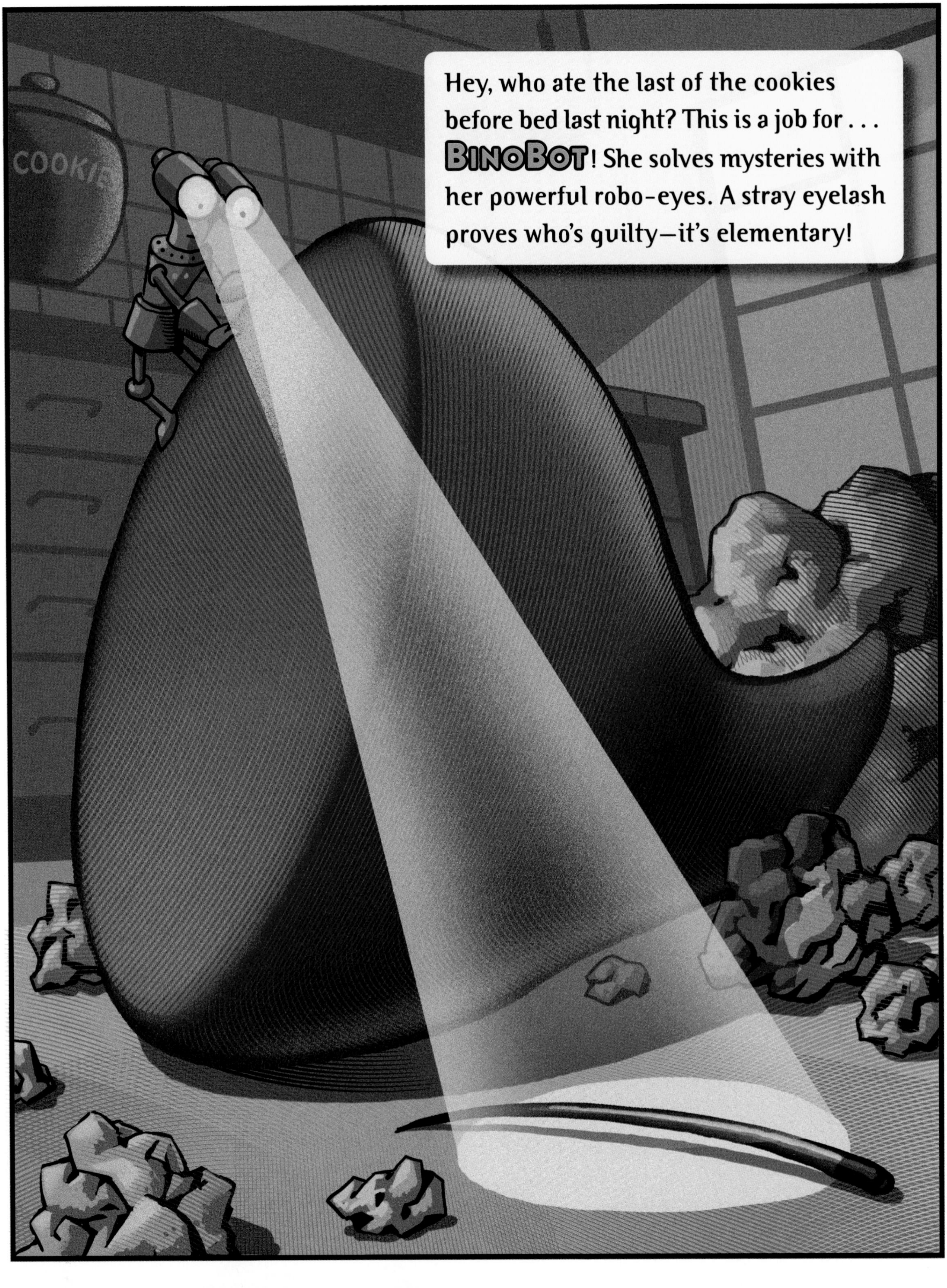
Hey, who ate the last of the cookies before bed last night? This is a job for . . . BINOBOT! She solves mysteries with her powerful robo-eyes. A stray eyelash proves who's guilty—it's elementary!
COOKIE

Good luck finding a **NANO-NANOBOT**! They're the smallest of them all. They live in a world so miniature, you'd need a very powerful microscope to see them. They're the best construction workers in the universe. They can build a car made from water and a house made from air (but they still like to play games, too).

The inventor was very proud that machines so small could do so much to help. "It's time to share the NanoBots with the world," he thought, and put them in a nano-sized box he'd made just for them. "The NanoBots will amaze them all!" he cried. Then he carried them to a very important show.

The inventor entered the NanoBots in a contest for Best New Invention, and displayed them in the crowded hall full of other clever experiments. But towering over the NanoBots was the most *GIANT* robot they had ever seen. The little machines began to feel very, very small.

GROW YOUR OWN HAND!

JUST ADD WATER!

Send Your Cat TO MEOW-TER SPACE

TAME YOUR MAN-EATING PLANT

SHARKS THE PETS OF THE FUTURE!

Cooking with Dinosaur Eggs

EXPLOSIONS THAT ARE Safe & Fun!

Grow 'em! Crack 'em! Eat 'em!

But the Big Bot was worried, too. His parts didn't fit, he kept falling from his chair, and his head seemed like it was ready to come off. "I am broken," said Big Bot. The NanoBots made excited robot sounds and raced to help.

The **GuardoBots** created a force field.
Lady Lance-o-Bot kept foreign invaders away.
The **SeekerBots** checked for nasty hidden creatures.
MediBot climbed into the nose to diagnose the problem.
BinoBot spied the broken wires.
The **MechanoBots** fixed the bad connections.
The **HeloBots** formed a cast for the wobbly leg.
The **ChewBots** devoured the leaking oil.
The **Nano-NanoBots** created some shiny new parts.

Big Bot hadn't just been repaired. He didn't just look brand-new. He stood taller than ever, and he looked truly *AWESOME*! The judges were amazed.

When they approached the NanoBot display, the great inventor exclaimed, "Ta-daaa!" The judges squinted their eyes, raised their eyebrows, and scratched their heads. The box seemed to be empty!

The NanoBots were too small to be seen. But they were proud to have done their jobs so well, and Big Bot was very grateful. When he won the prize, the NanoBots received an even better reward: the huge smile on his face. It made them very happy, even if the smile was made of tape.

And though the great inventor was disappointed that the NanoBots didn't win, they built him something that made him feel much better.
But suddenly, they realized they had a problem. MEDIBOT was still stuck inside Big Bot!

Luckily, **MEDIBOT** knew just where to tickle . . .

ACHOO!

. . . and Big Bot sneezed with a mighty mechanical roar.

And the next day, the NanoBots learned that even greater adventures lay ahead of them. They were small, but right now they were feeling *VERY BIG!*

MISSION OF THE DAY
- CURE THE SICK
- CLEAN UP OIL SPILL
- PROTECT CROPS
- SERVE HUMANKIND
- HAVE FUN

THE WORLD OF NANO-ROBOTICS

Nano-robotics is the science of creating machinery at the "nanoscale" of size. "Nano" refers to *one-billionth* of something. A nanometer, for example, is one-billionth of a meter—in other words, very, very small.* The first micromachine, invented in 1960, was an electric motor smaller than the head of a pin, and since then there have been great advances in this technology. While the future of nano-robotics is largely theoretical, scientists estimate that within five to twenty years, much of the potential suggested in this book may become reality.

Medicine: Within a few years, nano-robots may be able to cure diseases. They could have the power to destroy individual "bad" cells, such as cancer cells, with great precision. Nanos might even be programmed to repair damaged tissue, like a million tiny surgeons operating all at once.

Industry: Because of their extremely small size, nano-robots could be able to repair complex electronics and computer chips and to manufacture precision machine parts that are currently impossible to make.

Environment: Enormous teams of nano-robots could be programmed to eliminate toxic waste spills by breaking down chemical bonds and rendering the spills harmless.

Exploration: While exploring the microscopic world, nano-robots could carry miniature cameras that transmit pictures to scientists. Like single-celled organisms, these nano-robots would propel themselves with a long whip called a *flagellum*.

Swarming: Small helicopters have already been invented that can fly together in elaborate formations, using computer "brains" to communicate. Drawing from insect behavior, these clouds of "smart dust" could be programmed to form shapes, such as protective barriers.

The possible uses for nano-robotics are limited only by the imagination! Nano-robots no bigger than a few atoms or molecules could have the ability to manipulate matter at the atomic scale, change DNA, or create a limitless variety of objects or materials. This could change the world in ways that have not yet been envisioned. While the idea of self-replicating, autonomous robots sounds like science fiction, the reality could be closer than we think. Such creations must remain under the control of those who design and program them.

* In reality, scientists may design nano-robots of any scale they wish, and because of that flexibility, liberties have been taken with the sizes of and the proportional relationships between the characters in this story. In order to better illustrate the tasks that such machines might perform, their scale has sometimes been adjusted for stronger visual storytelling.